ONE POTATO,
TWO POTATO,
Three Potato,
Four

ONE POTATO,
TWO POTATO,
Three Potato,
Four

Edited by Bernagh Brims

Illustrated by Duncan Smith

Appletree Press

First published in 1990 by the Appletree Press Ltd,
7 James Street South, Belfast BT2 8DL

This collection © The Appletree Press Ltd, 1990
Illustrations © Duncan Smith, 1990

The publisher gratefully acknowledges the
financial assistance of the Northern Bank Ltd

**British Library Cataloguing in Publication
Data**
Brims, Bernagh
One potato, two potato,
three potato, four.
1. Children's short stories in English – Antholo-
gies
I. Title II. Smith, Duncan *1957*–
823.01089282 [J]

ISBN 0-86281-259-3

Contents

THE ZONKEY THAT NEVER WAS

Jennifer McCully

On a farm in County Antrim, quite near Glenariff, lived a little donkey called Archie. Now, although he was only small he had a GREAT BIG WISH – that when he grew up he would become a zebra. He had once seen a picture of one and ever since had longed to have a beautiful black and white striped suit, just like a zebra's.

'Far nicer than my plain grey one,' he muttered to himself. 'Ah well, I don't think I'll have too long to wait now. I'll soon be grown up and *then* I'll be a zebra.'

'You shouldn't be in such a hurry to grow up, Archie,' his Mummy often said to him, 'and you know it *is* a bit daft of you to think that when you're big you'll become a zebra.

You're a donkey, and even when you're big you'll *still* be a donkey. You're never going to turn into a zebra.'

'Yes I will,' argued Archie. 'Sure amn't I just like one now? All that's missing is the stripes and they'll appear once I get a bit older. Just you wait and see.'

'What's the use of talking to the silly wee thing,' sighed his Mummy, but she loved him just the same.

All the other animals on the farm knew about Archie and his big wish, and they made terrible fun of him – but he didn't care one bit.

'Have you ever thought of using a drop of paint?' asked a very helpful cow one morning, when they were having a bit of a yarn over the hedge.

'I saw some large tins of black and white paint sitting near the farmhouse when I was going to the byre for the milking. You could

put some lovely stripes on yourself with that.'

'The very thing,' said Archie excitedly, and off he galloped like a shot. Sure enough, there were the tins of paint just as the cow had said.

'Oh dear, there's no striped stuff,' said Archie in a disappointed voice. 'Ah well, maybe I can mix them.'

With a struggle he hooked his tail through the handle of the black tin and managed to heave it off the ground, but when he tried to

tip it up the whole thing slipped, there was a tremendous crash and an ocean of black paint crept slowly across the farmyard. The farmer came racing out to see what had happened and when his eyes lit on the ghastly mess he was fit to be tied.

'That stupid beast!' he roared. 'Just look what he's done now. Come Lammas-tide I'll pack him off to the fair at Ballycastle, just you see if I don't.'

Poor Archie. All he had to show for his

efforts was a rather streaky looking tail.

Then, one day, he heard the farmer and his wife planning to take their children to the Wildlife Park up at Dervock.

'Why, that's it,' he whispered to himself excitedly. 'Why didn't I think of that before? I bet they have zebras there, and one of them is bound to have a set of stripes to spare.'I'm all set now – I'm going to run away from home and go to the Wildlife Park.'

And so he did. The very next morning, very

11

early, he tiptoed away from his Mummy, got out of the field and set off for the Park. The only problem was, he hadn't the faintest idea which direction he should go, so he took the first road that came to hand. He walked a very long way but seemed to be getting nowhere in particular and at last, feeling very tired and cross he sat down to rest under a whin bush. A rabbit poked its head out of a near-by hole and looked at him curiously.

'Hello,' he said. 'Where are you going little donkey?'

'I'm *not* a donkey,' answered Archie crossly. 'I'm a zebra.'

'Oh, really,' said the rabbit. 'I always thought zebras had stripes. What's happened to yours – have they had an accident?'

'Er – um – I've – er – lost them,' snapped Archie. 'As a matter of fact I'm just walking along here trying to find them. They must have dropped off when I wasn't looking. *You* haven't seen a set of stripes lying about anywhere, have you?'

'What blethers,' laughed the rabbit. 'Fallen off, my foot. You aren't fooling me one bit, you're a donkey, so don't try telling me you're really a zebra with his stripes dropped off. Ho! Ho! Ho! I never heard anything like it.' And

he disappeared back down into his burrow, still laughing.

Feeling rather silly, Archie got up and walked off. He was also a bit frightened as he had never been away from home before. He walked on a bit further and finally came to a town. It was Cushendun. The noise of the traffic made him feel even more frightened. When he tried to cross the road he couldn't because the cars wouldn't stop for him. Then he saw a group of people who also seemed to be trying to get across, so Archie went up and stood behind them. Just in front of him was a little boy and his Mummy.

'Now remember,' Archie heard her explain to the little boy, 'we are crossing the road here because this is a safe crossing place. It's called a zebra crossing, and you should always use one if you want to cross the road.'

'But how do you know where there *is* a zebra crossing?' asked the little boy.

'Well,' answered his Mummy, 'you'll always know them by the black and white stripes on the road.'

Just then everyone started to walk across and Archie went with them.

'What's all this about zebras crossing?' he thought to himself. He looked all round to see if he could spot one. 'I don't see any zebras.' Then he happened to look down at the ground and the awful sight that he saw made him freeze with fright.

'My goodness,' he said. 'It can't be – it *is*! It's zebra skins all over the road, and people are trampling about on top of them. How horrible. So that's what the lady meant when she was talking about zebra crossings, and *that's* what they do with zebras when they get old. They skin them and put their skins on the road for people to walk on. Right, that's it. I'm going home to my Mummy.'

He turned as quickly as he could and didn't

stop galloping until he had reached his own field where his Mummy was looking very worried. 'My goodness, Archie,' she said, racing over to him at once. 'Where on earth have you been? I've been worried stiff about you.'

'Oh Mummy,' gasped Archie as soon as he saw her, 'You'll never guess the awful thing that I've just found out ...'

And so Archie told his Mummy the whole story, and all about what he had seen, and how people use zebra skins to put on the road.

'You are the silliest little donkey I've ever seen,' laughed his Mummy when Archie had finished his story. 'Those weren't *real* zebra skins, they were just black and white stripes painted on the road so that people will know where there is a safe place to cross. They're called 'zebra crossings' because they're the same colour as a zebra's stripes.'

Well, she had a really hard job to make

Archie believe her, and even yet he's none too sure. But it certainly put an end to his big wish, for he had had such a fright that he decided that perhaps being a donkey wasn't so bad after all and he'd just be content to stay plain grey!

SAM MAKES UP HIS MIND

Linda Barclay

Sam was thinking very hard. It was his sixth birthday and the one thing that was making him think so deeply was – what was he going to choose for his birthday present from his Mum and Dad? He hated having to choose between lots of different things. It was such hard work because he could never make up his mind. He was always afraid he'd choose the wrong thing.

Sometimes he made people a bit cross with him because, when they asked him what he wanted to do, or where he wanted to go, or what he'd like to eat, he'd just stand there and say nothing, thinking hard and trying to decide. He simply could *not* make up his mind.

Take yesterday afternoon for example. His Mum had called to him, 'Sam, I'm getting the potatoes ready for tea! Do you want them mashed or boiled or fried? Would you like chips or potato pie? What about roast ones? Or creamed? Hurry up and choose dear!'

Sam didn't mind what way he had his potatoes really, but he did like chips. When he'd said, 'Chips, please', his Mum had said, 'You always choose chips, let's have boiled tonight.' He couldn't win.

Even this morning at breakfast he had to choose what sort of eggs to have. His Mum had said, 'Do you want them scrambled, or fried or poached? Would you like them soft? How about runny with toast? What about hard-boiled or an omelette? Hurry up and choose Sam!' Sam couldn't make up his mind. There were so many ways he liked eggs. When he said nothing, because he was thinking hard about what to choose, his Mum gave him a poached one, when really he wouldn't have minded a boiled one or even a fried one. Oh dear, it was difficult!

Now it was his birthday and he had to choose a present. Most boys and girls look forward to choosing a present but not Sam. He *couldn't* make up his mind. His Dad had started already, trying to help him choose. He'd said: 'What kind of present would you like, Sam? How about a cricket bat? What about a ball? You like books, Sam, but you'd have to choose which one. How about a track suit? What about some Lego? You're going to have to choose, Sam, it's your birthday today!'

Sam and his Mum and Dad set off for the shops, and all the while they walked Sam kept thinking about what he would choose. His Mum and Dad asked him again and in the end he said, 'A ball.'

They looked in a shop window. His Mum said, 'Would you like a blue ball or a red ball or a green one? Would you like that spotty one? Or what about that stripy one at the back? Do you want a football? Or a tennis ball? Or a rubber ball? Would you like a large or a small one? What sort of ball, Sam?'

Sam *couldn't* decide, so they left the shop to think about it.

As they walked, they came to the pet shop at Smithfield and stopped to look at the animals in the windows. There were goldfish swimming round in bowls, opening and closing their mouths the way fish do, and budgies in cages looking at themselves in little mirrors, and there

were white mice running round and round little wheels, and kittens licking their paws.

But Sam's eyes lit on the puppies. He couldn't take his eyes off them. There were four of them, round and fat and roly-poly, with

little pink tongues and waggly tails. As Sam was laughing at them, one of the pups came right up to the window, and put out its tongue at Sam and stood on its back legs scratching the window at him, trying to get out.

Sam looked at the pup and smiled and looked some more and then he turned to his Mum and Dad and said: 'I *know* what I want! See that wee, black pup there, that one at the front? I'd like *him* please. It's great, I didn't choose him. He chose me!'

So Sam got just the present he wanted and after that he got much better at choosing. He chose a lead for the puppy and he chose a name. He called his pup Smithy, because he got him in Smithfield.

WINNIE THE WITCH

Albert Crawford

It was a fine crisp day, the very last day of October, and Winnie the Witch was feeling very happy, for this was the night of the Hallowe'en Witches' Ball. It was always great fun and Winnie looked forward to it every year. This year, however, she was just a little bit worried for the Head Witch had made a new rule and this was it.

'All witches must frighten someone or they will not be allowed into the Ball.'

Now you see, our Winnie was badly out of practice at frightening anything for she liked everything. She liked children, grown-ups, birds and every living creature in the wild woods and she did not want to frighten any of them. Still, she had to do it, so she straightened her pointed hat on her sticking-out hair and said to a robin on a twig.

'Well, if I must, I must. I just have to get into that Ball, so I'm off to frighten somebody.' Then, she picked up her broom, called to Nick, her black cat, and set off.

Now she had not gone far before she met Farmer Higgins clipping his hedge.

'Ah,' she thought, 'he will do very nicely. I'll only give him a tiny little frighten.'

Winnie took a big breath, screwed up her face, stuck out her teeth, crossed her eyes and

jumped out in front of Farmer Higgins with a scream and a screech.

Farmer Higgins swung round from his clipping and when he saw the screwed-up face, the crossed eyes and the sticking-out teeth, he just burst out laughing. He laughed and he laughed, and he doubled up and he laughed, till the tears ran down his red cheeks.

'Oh Winnie,' he gasped, 'you do look funny with that twisted-up face. Oh dear, maybe I shouldn't laugh. Is it your sore back? Is it Winnie? Is your back bad again? Oh dear, I am sorry.'

Winnie put on her ordinary face and said with a sigh, 'Och are you not terrified, Farmer Higgins? Are you not trembling in your wellies?'

Well, Farmer Higgins gave such a roar of laughter that it was a few minutes before he could speak. Then at last, he said, 'Frightened? Scared? Trembling in my wellies? Why

Winnie, I could never be frightened of you. Sure, we all love you round here. Frightened of our Winnie!' and he had another fit of laughing.

Winnie turned away and went on down the road, not at all pleased with her first try at frightening. 'Oh well, she said. It's still early. I'll soon find someone to frighten.'

She looked down at Nick, her cat, trotting beside her.

'Mind you,' she told him, 'I want to get this frightening bit over for I have to get my hair done-over spiky and my Sunday black hat starched. I cannot go to the Ball with a droopy hat.'

Suddenly, Winnie heard another sound. She stopped and listened. 'Why, it's a baby crying,' she said to Nick and, turning a corner, they saw Mrs Brown's baby in his pram outside the front window. Winnie stopped and rubbed her long chin.

'I wonder,' she said softly. 'I wonder.' She crept closer.

'Surely a teeny weeny little frighten wouldn't do any harm. Little Timmy is crying anyway and sure if I gave him the teeniest, weeniest scare, he might not even notice and then I would be allowed into the Ball.'

Gently she went close to the pram and screwing up her face just a tiny bit, she popped her head over the edge and said a very quiet, 'Boo.'

She was about to pull her head out again and hurry off, when Timmy opened his blue eyes and, can you guess what happened? Well, he stuck out one round, chubby hand and caught Winnie's nose and changed his crying

28

He stuck out one round, chubby hand.

to chuckles of laughter. Then he actually started laughing. Timmy chuckled and chortled and giggled and wriggled. He was now a real happy baby and what could poor Winnie do. She bent down and kissed him and tucked the white blanket around him.

'Ye wee rascal,' she smiled, but she knew she had failed again. She hadn't even been able to frighten a tiny baby.

As she went on her way, her head was in a whirl. Here she was, with her hair to do and her hat to starch and she had not frightened one single person, not even a little baby like Timmy. What was she going to do? She was so sad that she sat down on a tree-stump and began to cry, with Nick, her black cat, crying beside her.

Suddenly, she heard the sound of singing and, looking up, she saw her friend, Willie the Wizard, skipping and dancing along the road. When he saw her he stopped and stared.

'What's the matter, Winnie?' he asked. 'Why are you crying on such a clean crisp day and a Ball to go to tonight?'

Then Winnie told him the whole sad story about how she could not frighten Farmer Higgins or even little Timmy. Willie rubbed his long chin and said,

'Hmmm, we'll have to do something about that. I can't have our Winnie missing the Ball.' Then his face brightened.

'Ah! I have an idea, he said smiling. 'Just you leave everything to Willie. I'll be back in two blinks of Nick's eyes. You'll see.' Then he turned on his heel and disappeared down the road towards the village.

In the Main Street, Willie met a crowd of children, all dressed up for Hallowe'en. They had blackened faces and funny hats and were running from door to door, rattling the knockers and whistling through the letter-boxes.

'Here, children,' shouted Willie, 'will you

do me a good turn?' When they saw that it was a real live Wizard, they rushed over and gathered round him.

'Now,' he began, 'you all know Winnie and, of course, she would never frighten anybody.' And all the children nodded their heads.

'Well, if she doesn't frighten someone to-day,' he went on, 'she cannot go to the Ball tonight. Now, here's what I want you to do. Just let me put a nice Wizardy Spell on you so that you will be just a teenzy weenzy bit frightened when we meet her. Will you come and do that for poor Winnie?'

Well, Willie did not have to ask twice. In less than two blinks of Nick's eyes, they were all dancing out of the village behind the Wizard and along the road. A real Wizard and a real spell, they thought. This was the best Hallowe'en they had ever had.

When Winnie heard the singing and laughing coming along the road, she just sniffed and sat there with her back to them. She was in no mood for singing or laughing.

A little way from her, Willie whispered, 'Halt,' and the whole band stopped. 'Now,' said Willie quietly, 'gather round till I get you spelled. William, stop giggling. Wizards can't get children spelled if they are laughing at them. This is serious stuff.'

The children stopped giggling and, stretching out his arms, Willie began:

By my pointed Wizard's hat,
By old Nick, the jet black cat,
By the magic powers in me,
When wee Winnie's face you see,
All you children here tonight,
Will howl and scream and run with fright!

When he was done, there was not a single

*The children stopped giggling and, stretching
out his arms, Willie began.*

giggle from anyone. All the boys and girls just stood quietly in a row behind Winnie. Then Willie tapped her on the shoulder.

'Come now, Winnie,' he said. 'Here's the children from the village. Now's your chance. Surely you'll be able to frighten at least one of them. Come on, give it your best frightener face.'

Winnie stopped sniffing and wiped her eyes on her big, wide sleeve. Then she took a great big breath and began:

She twisted her mouth into a question mark;

Hooked up her nose till it looked like a coat-peg;

Stuck out her ears till she looked like a donkey;

Stuck out her teeth till she looked like a rabbit;

Rolled her eyes till she looked like a fruit-machine at the seaside;

Then, with one great leap, she whirled round on the children and screamed:

Crashing thunder, flashing light,
Am I not an awful sight?
Look upon this frightful face
Then away in fear you race.

Some of the boys and girls felt they wanted to laugh, but there was another feeling in them as well. Their feet wanted to run, for the Wizard's spell was working. Then, all at once, every little foot turned and, with every little mouth squealing as in the school playground at lunchtime, the whole crowd took to their heels and raced for the village. To this very day, they still talk about that wonderful Hallowe'en with a real Wizard and a real Witch.

Winnie was so pleased. She turned her face back to the kind one she always had and smiled up at Willie. Then the pair of them linked arms and danced off down the road towards her cottage to get ready for the Witches' Hallowe'en Ball.

*Roly Boley was knocking an apple off
the highest branch in an apple-tree.*

THE HOLESTONE

Hendy Foy

Once upon a time, in a thick forest near Doagh, Roly Boley was knocking an apple off the highest branch in an apple-tree ... with his NOSE! Like all Boleys, Roly had a very, VERY, V E R Y long nose, nearly as long as a lamp post. Apples are a Boley's favourite food, so you can see their big, long noses came in very handy.

Roly picked the apple up and started to munch it.

'Ah, lovely,' he said. He saw his sister, Rosy Boley, carrying a very large sheet of paper.

'What have you there?' asked Roly.

'Oh, Roly, it's a notice from Old Boley and it says the time has come to choose a new King,' answered Rosy.

'Hmmmfh! Nothing to do with me, Rosy,'

said Roly. 'Apples are much more important than Kings.' Roly was a very greedy Boley.

'Ah, but you know that the Boley King is always the Boley with the longest nose' said Rosy. 'Well, Paddy Boley, who lives beside the big chestnut tree, has one of the two longest noses in Boleyland and guess who has the other one?'

'Dunno!' said Roly. 'And don't care!'

'Well, you'd better care, Roly, because *you* have the other longest nose ... Either you or Paddy is going to be the new King, whichever of you has the longest nose.'

'Me ... it'll be ME. I'll make a brilliant King. I'm sure my nose is bigger than Paddy's. I eat more apples than Paddy so mine must be longer!' said Roly, who wanted to be the best at everything.

'You'd better knock down more apples and eat them quickly,' laughed Rosy, 'because the contest to find who has the largest Boley nose will be tomorrow. Everyone is to meet at the Boley Holestone to decide who will be the new King.'

Meanwhile, in a house beside the big chestnut tree, Paddy Boley was lying in bed. He was reading about the contest to find the new King too. Poor Paddy had a dreadful cold. He could feel a sneeze coming on. 'Ah ... Ah ... AH ...' Boley noses were so long that they had to cut a hole in the ceilings of their bedrooms so that when they went to bed their noses could stick right out through the roof. Out in the air, a Boleybird flew down and perched on Paddy's nose.

'Ah ... AH ... TCHOOOOOO!' The poor Boleybird had an awful fright and flew off in a hurry.

'I do hobe my nobe ib bigger than Roley's. Oh, I'm ture it ib,' said Paddy. He couldn't

speak properly with his bad cold. He had to spend most of the day in bed and when he was dressing the next day to go to the Boley Holestone, his cold was no better.

But Roly Boley couldn't wait for the contest. He was sure his nose was the longest. He asked Rosy to make sure his hair was looking neat before he set off for the Holestone.

At the Boley Holestone a big crowd was gathering and everyone was excited. The Boley cooks were making apple dumplings and apple chutney and apple pies and stewed apples and litres of apple juice for the feast. Boley boys from Ballyeaston were putting up flags and Boley girls from Ballynure were practising their music because they were in the Boley Band. There were even a few bad Boley boys writing on the tree trunks PADDY FOR KING and ROLY WILL WEAR THE CROWN.

At the top of the hill stood the Boley Holestone. It was an enormous stone standing on its end, as tall as a man and with a small hole right through it. The new King was to be chosen the way all Boley Kings are chosen, by sticking his nose through the hole in the Boley Holestone. The bit of his nose sticking through the hole is measured and the Boley with the longest will be King. The oldest Boley there, Old Boley, told everyone to be quiet. The contest was about to begin.

First, he called Roly Boley up to the Holestone.

'Hurrah,' cheered all Roly's friends, and his sister Rosy.

Old Boley told Roly to stick his nose through the hole in the Holestone. The crowd was silent as Old Boley took a Boleystick and measured Roly's nose.

'Ladies and gentlemen,' said Old Boley, 'I have measured Roly's nose and it is NINE BOLEY STICKS LONG.'

'Hurrah,' went the crowd. They all gave

Paddy a big cheer too, when Old Boley called him up to the Holestone. Everyone liked him and they knew about his terrible cold. Paddy pushed his nose through the hole in the Holestone, and Old Boley measured the end sticking out of the hole.

'Friends,' announced Old Boley. 'I have measured Paddy's nose and it is also NINE BOLEY STICKS LONG!'

'What are we going to do? We can't have

two Kings. There's nothing about that in the rulebook!'

Just then Paddy felt a sneeze coming ... a big sneeze ... perhaps the BIGGEST SNEEZE since he caught the cold. When the crowd realised that Paddy was going to sneeze, they all dived for cover behind the trees. It was a good idea because Paddy sneezed the biggest, wettest, noisiest sneeze of his entire life. 'AHHHHHHHHH ... C H O O O O O O O O !'

Such a sneeze! Poor Paddy ... he had sneezed so hard that his nose swelled – and stuck tight in the Boley Holestone. Everyone came out from behind the trees where they had taken shelter and gathered round.

'My nobe ib tuck!' cried Paddy.

Old Boley tried to pull him out but he couldn't, so he asked for a strong rope and seven strong Boleys. The rope was tied around Paddy's waist and the seven strong Boleys pulled and PULLED and P U L L E D and at last Paddy's nose popped out of the hole and Paddy landed with a thump on the grass. Paddy's nose was all scraped and sore, but ... as far as old Boley and the seven strong Boleys could see ... all that pulling and stretching had made Paddy's nose longer!

Old Boley told Paddy to stick his nose through the hole in the Holestone once again. Old Boley took the Boley Stick and measured Paddy's nose ... then cleared his throat and shouted, 'Quiet everyone! Paddy's nose has been measured for a second time and this time it is TEN BOLEY STICKS LONG! PADDY'S NOSE IS THE LONGEST! WE HAVE A NEW KING!'

'Hurrah!'

The crowd was delighted and clapped until their hands were sore. The Boley Band started to play and everyone made their way to the feast. Roly Boley didn't look too happy as he bit into a large apple but King Paddy Boley had a huge smile as Old Boley put on his crown. Old Boley also put a large bandage on the end of Paddy's sore nose, and tied it up with a red ribbon. He felt a bit silly but it didn't stop him tucking into a very big bowl of apple dumpling and as he did Old Boley shouted, 'THREE CHEERS FOR PADDY BOLEY ... THE NEW KING! HIP! HIP! ... HORRAY!'

Maybe you can visit the Holestone near Ballyclare sometime!

THE PIPER

retold by Barbara Gray

It was a lovely warm afternoon towards the end of September. Three men came walking along the road, wearing old trousers and open-necked shirts, and each of them carrying a bundle containing the rest of his belongings – a change of clothes, a piece of soap and a razor for shaving with, and some money to take home.

They had been working on a farm in County Antrim, but the harvest was all gathered in and their work was done. The farmer didn't need them to help him during the winter, so they had packed up their bundles and were now on the long walk home to County Fermanagh.

It was a long way and after a while, they

began to feel very tired, and thought they had better stop for a rest. They lay back against the grassy bank by the side of the road, and almost dozed off in the warm sun.

'Here's someone coming along the road,' said one of the men. 'He'll be company for us, if he's going our way.'

As the man got nearer, they could see him properly. He was a strange little man, with a bushy beard and a big mop of black, curly hair beneath his old cloth cap. He was wearing a very worn waistcoat and an old shirt and trousers that had been patched a few times and he was carrying a set of uilleann pipes.

'Good evening to you, gentlemen,' he said. 'Are you all feeling tired?'

'Indeed we are. We've been working all summer on a big farm in Cloughmills, and now we have to walk all the way home to County Fermanagh.'

*He was a strange little man with a bushy
beard and a big mop of black, curly hair
beneath his old cloth cap.*

'County Fermanagh? That's a long walk indeed, but if you like, I'll go part of the way with you, and I'll play some music to keep a spring in your step.'

So off they set once more, and it made such a difference going along to the cheerful music, as the piper skipped along ahead of them. A little further on, the piper stopped. There, right in the middle of the road, lay an old pair of boots.

'That's a bit of luck,' said the piper. 'Just what I could do with. They might be old, but they're not as old as the ones I'm wearing. Look! They've been mended more times than I can remember.'

'Here, I'll carry the boots for you in my bundle,' said one of the men, 'and then you'll still have your hands free to play the pipes.'

So they went on again, carrying the boots with them. They got as far as Templepatrick, and as it was getting dark, they thought they had better find somewhere to spend the night. At the next farmhouse they came to, the four men asked if there would be any room for them, and the farmer's wife invited them in.

'I'll make you a good supper, and you can sleep in the barn for tonight,' she said kindly.

Out they went to the barn, and the farmer followed, carrying a few old blankets for them.

'You'll be all right here,' he said, 'but one word of warning – stay away from the grey cow there. She eats just about everything she can reach. She'd eat the very coat off your back!'

But the men were so tired, they didn't worry too much. They just fell asleep immediately and the poor old cow didn't get a wink of sleep, because one of them snored so loudly.

Early the next morning, the piper woke up, and had a great big stretch and a yawn.

'It's time I was off. I've helped these men on their way, but I've work to do.'

The other men were still asleep, so the piper folded up his blanket nice and neatly, and tip-toed over to the men's bundles and found his boots.

'They're a lot better than my old ones,' he said, and put them on. 'And a great fit, too!'

The cow opened one eye and looked at him.

'I hope you haven't got your eye on my new boots,' laughed the piper. 'I'll tell you what ... I'll leave you my old ones!'

He left his old boots sitting beside his folded blanket and went on his way.

The cow mooed loudly and the other men woke up with a jump. Just as the piper had done, they yawned and stretched. They were not looking forward to another long day's walking.

Just then, the farmer's wife appeared with

breakfast for them.

'I see you're all right, then,' she said. 'No trouble from the cow? I'll just leave a bit of breakfast for you over here. Oh, no!'

She cried out so loudly it made the men jump.

'The piper. Where's the piper?'

They all looked round, but there was no sign of him. The farmer's wife had spotted his old boots beside the blanket.

'Oh, no! Only his boots are left!'

She called for the farmer.

'Come quickly, come quickly! The old grey cow has eaten the piper! Only his boots are left!'

The farmer came running in as fast as his legs would carry him.

'The cow has eaten the piper! Oh, what are we to do?' cried the poor woman.

Everybody looked very shocked, but the cow just watched them all, with a twinkle in her eye

'If I didn't need you for the milk, I'd have you made into sausages!' the farmer told her, but she just said 'MOO' and didn't look at all worried.

The three men couldn't understand it. If the cow really had eaten the piper, surely they would have heard a lot of noise and fuss. On the other hand, if the cow hadn't eaten the piper, where could he be? They wouldn't have thought that he would just leave without saying goodbye and without even waiting for his breakfast.

Speaking of breakfast, they were feeling rather hungry, and the breakfast the farmer's wife had brought looked very tasty. They began to eat, still wondering what could have happened to the piper.

'This will be a good story to tell,' they said, 'but I don't suppose anybody will ever believe us.'

The farmer was very worried. Well, can you imagine having to explain that your cow ate a person who was sleeping in your barn?

'I'm sure you didn't earn enough money working on the farm,' he said. 'If I was to give you some money would you keep this a secret?'

Since the men didn't really know what had happened to the piper anyway, they agreed, took the money and promised not to tell. The farmer watched them leave, and kept his fingers crossed that they would keep their promise.

The three men set off on their journey again, talking about what had happened. They had

had a lucky escape if the cow had really eaten the piper! And then, turning a bend in the road, who did they see ahead of them but a strange little figure in old clothes and not so old boots, dancing along in time to the music of his pipes ...

THE TWELVE MONTHS OF THE YEAR

retold by Felicity Hayes-McCoy

Once upon a time, not my time and not your time either, but a very good time all the same, there were two sisters whose names were Cathleen and Noreen. And they lived in a cottage in a deep valley in the middle of the Sperrin mountains.

Now Cathleen was a cheerful girl who smiled when good fortune came to her friends. But Noreen was an angry girl who was jealous of everybody.

One morning, when all the birds were singing, Cathleen set out along the winding path that led from the cottage to the mountains. And it wasn't long before she came to bare rocks where nothing grew but heather and golden whin.

Then, suddenly, a cloud passed the sun and

the birds stopped singing. And Cathleen saw a deep, dark cave that she'd never seen before. Inside was firelight, glowing and flickering. So in she walked to see what she could see.

And what should she find but twelve old women, sitting round the fire doing nothing at all.

Each old woman wore a long grey robe which covered her from head to toe. And one of them raised her head and spoke to Cathleen.

'You're welcome, Cathleen,' she said, 'and we're pleased to see you. Shove round there now, sisters,' she said to the others, 'and give the wee girl room to sit down.'

So all the old women shuffled and wriggled and made a place for Cathleen by the fire. And then Cathleen thanked them and sat down.

And the old woman spoke again.

'Well, now, Cathleen,' she said. 'Here's a question for you. Tell me this and tell me no more, what do you think of the twelve months of the year?'

Then all the old women held their breaths. And Cathleen smiled.

'March, April and May,' she said. 'Those are the months of spring when the earth wakes up and the buds begin to shoot. I do always think springtime is like a new beginning.'

'So it is, Cathleen, so it is,' said the old

woman.

And three of her sisters sat back, well satisfied.

Then Cathleen spoke again.

'June is the cherry month,' she said, 'and in July the corn begins to shoot. Then comes August when the fields all turn to gold. Everyone loves the summer.'

'So they do, Cathleen, so they do,' said the old woman.

And three more of her sisters sat back, well satisfied.

Then Cathleen spoke again.

'September is the flaming month when the leaves are scarlet and bronze. And in October, after the harvest, there's barmbrack and bonfires and games. November days are short, of course, but there's firelight and the smell of roast apples. So sometimes I think autumn is the best season of all.'

'So you do, Cathleen, so you do,' said the old woman.

And another three sisters sat back, well satisfied.

'Then there's winter,' said Cathleen. 'And winter's a wonderful time. December is the Christ Child's month when we celebrate His birth. In January the frost turns the grass to shining spears. The February winds bring the smell of the wakening earth. And after that it's March again and we start another year. So I suppose,' she said, 'that I'm happy with every month God sends us.'

'So you are, Cathleen, so you are,' said the old woman.

And all twelve sisters sat back, smiling and well satisfied.

Then the old woman spoke again.

'Well, Cathleen, you've answered us kindly,' she said, 'and my sisters and I would like to give you a present. Reach out now, daughter, and fill up your apron with coals from our fire.'

Then Cathleen slowly reached out one hand to the flames. And, to her delight, she found that the fiery coals neither burnt her fingers nor scorched her apron. So she gathered a great pile of them and, when she had thanked the old women, she set off home again, carefully holding her apron by the corners.

As soon as she reached the cottage she called out loudly.

'Noreen, Noreen, see what I've got.' And she shook out her apron to show her fiery present.

She saw a shower of gold falling from the apron.

But when Noreen came running, instead of glowing coals, she saw a shower of gold falling from the apron and gleaming and glinting on the kitchen floor.

When Noreen heard the story she was so envious she could hardly speak. And then she had an idea.

'I'll go up the mountain myself,' she said, 'and get my share of what's going.'

So the very next morning, as soon as it was light, off she went in her biggest apron.

It wasn't long before she came to the cave and the twelve old women seated round the fire.

'You're welcome, Noreen,' said the old woman who had spoken to Cathleen, 'and we're pleased to see you.'

But before she could say any more, Noreen had pushed past her to the fire and sat down in front of it.

'Right,' she said, 'so you want to know what I think of the twelve months of the year?'

The twelve old women looked at each other strangely. But Noreen went on and never noticed.

'First there's March, April and May,' she said. 'I hate them. The cherry blossom gets everywhere and I'm the one who has to clean it up. Spring's a dirty season, I've always said so.'

'So you have, Noreen, so you have,' said the old woman.

And three of her sisters sat back, dissatisfied.

'June, July and August,' said Noreen. 'There's sweaty, tiresome months for you. Flies buzzing and wasps stinging and hours spent working in the sun. I feel bad tempered all summer long, so I do.'

'So you do, Noreen, so you do,' said the old

woman.

And three more of her sisters sat back, dissatisfied.

'Then there's the autumn months,' said Noreen crossly, 'September, October and November. There's apples in the barrels and corn in the barns and none of it belongs to me. Oh, I'm envious of my neighbours in autumn, so I am.'

'So you are, Noreen, so you are,' said the old woman.

And another three sisters sat back, dissatisfied.

'As for the winter,' said Noreen, 'that's worst of all. December's cold, January's dark and February's soaking wet. I think I'm more miserable in winter than at any other time of the year,' she said, 'and that's saying a lot.'

'So it is, Noreen, so it is,' said the old woman.

And all twelve sisters sat back, dissatisfied.

Then the old woman spoke again and she never smiled at all.

'You've told us what you think,' she said. 'Now here is your reward.'

And she told Noreen to fill up her apron with coals from the fire.

Well, Noreen didn't stop to thank her. She piled as many coals as she could into her apron and she rushed out of the cave, down the mountain, across the valley and into the cottage.

She could hardly wait to see the shower of gold fall gleaming and glinting to the kitchen floor.

But as soon as she let go the corners of her apron she began to scream and stamp in rage. For, instead of gold, a shower of hopping, green frogs fell down behind the dresser, under the table and into the settle bed.

They hopped and they jumped and they bounced and they danced, up and down the stairs, round and round the oven and in and out of every room in the cottage.

And if they're not gone yet she is chasing them still.

AMANDA SHORTLEGS

Martin Waddell

Once upon a time, when Belfast was a bit of sticky mud by the river and Derry was a grove of tiny oak trees, there was a very nasty giant named Cecil.

Cecil lived over Ballynahinch way. Every day he went out and ate peasants that he plucked from the bushes where they were hiding, the way someone else might pick blackberries.

All the peasants were terrified, except Mrs Ogle. Mrs Ogle sprang into action! She sent for her tiny daughter, Amanda Shortlegs Ogle, Amanda Shortlegs for short. 'Get rid of Cecil, Amanda!' she ordered. 'Oh Ma!' moaned Amanda. '*Now*, Amanda!' said Mrs Ogle.

Amanda got her hammer and chisel and cut out a notice on the biggest rock she could find, which was Scrabo. (The notice isn't there now, because a dinosaur from Comber rubbed against it one day.) The notice said:

WANTED

A HERO TO BASH CECIL

signed: Amanda Shortlegs

There were *lots* of heroes in Newtownards, and four of them came almost at once. Amanda signed them up at a goat a day, plus expenses. Goats were what they used for money then. (You could buy a cave in Antrim with a fitted kitchen for twenty goats down payment, and a kid a week.)

The heroes had some soda bread and honey to get their strength up, and then they charged off to bash Cecil.

BIFF–BANG–WALLOP!

Cecil duffed them up, and had Hero Hot

*Normally Esmerelda charged forty goats for getting
rid of giants and she was very insulted.*

Pot for tea. Mrs Ogle was very cross when Amanda told her. 'Do something at once, Amanda!' she said. 'Oh Ma!' sighed Amanda. '*Now*, Amanda,' said Mrs Ogle.

Amanda thought for a bit, and then she went to see Esmerelda, the Witch of the Woods, who lived up the Malone Road in Belfast, only Belfast wasn't there then, and the Malone Road was just a cow-path on the way to the Goat-Bank.

'How many goats will you pay me?' asked Esmerelda.

'A goat a day, plus expenses,' said Amanda, 'and a free pass for Ulsterbuses, when they are invented.'

Normally Esmerelda charged forty goats for getting rid of giants and she was *very* insulted. Esmerelda *almost* turned Amanda into a bus-stop. Amanda would have been the first bus-stop on the Malone Road, and very lonely too, because there were no buses then. (There aren't many now.) Amanda only just escaped, but she did.

Mrs Ogle was very, very angry. 'Don't *Oh Ma!* me, Amanda!' she said. 'Do something, *now!*'

Amanda sat there eating soda farls and honey and *thought*. When she had finished thinking she set off to carry out her Plan.

First of all, she dug and she dug with her dinosaur bone spade. She dug a Cecil Pit. She was a good digger, but she still couldn't dig a pit deep enough to trap Cecil, because he was too B I G.

That *wasn't* her Plan.

Next she went around the whole of County Down from Kilkeel to Bangor, whizzing about in her cow cart. It had to be a cow cart because Cecil had eaten the horses. She filled the cow cart up with all the honey she could find and when she got to the Cecil Pit, she tipped it all in. But the honey wasn't to drown Cecil in, because Cecil was too B I G.

That *wasn't* her Plan.

Then Amanda whirred off in her cow cart again, cow galloping from Carryduff to Millisle and round the Ards peninsula and up to Mourne, collecting all the beehives with the bees in them. Gallop–gallop–gallop went the cow and cart. It was the Fastest Cow Cart in the east and it had to be, because the bees were angry about losing their honey.

Amanda hid the beehives near the Cecil Pit, and then she banged on the hives to make sure the bees would buzz and then she hid herself with her Amanda Shortlegs Special Bee-Releaser. This was a bit of string tied to the bee-flaps, so she could open them all at once.

BUZZ–BUZZ–BUZZ

Cecil heard the buzzing, and he hopped over

The bees buzzed out, heading for Cecil and their stolen honey.

the Dromara hills from Banbridge, where he'd been having a bath in the Bann. Bees mean honey, and there was nothing Cecil liked better than a bit of honey on his toasted peasant.

SPLOSH!

Cecil fell in the Cecil Pit.

'AARRRRRRRRRH!' Cecil roared, climbing out of the Cecil Pit, dripping with honey and *then* ...

Amanda Shortlegs pulled her string.

The bees buzzed out, heading for Cecil and their stolen honey.

'AAAAAAAAAA!' screeched Cecil.

'OOOOOOOOOO!' yelled Cccil.

'MUMMY–MUMMY–MUMMY!' howled Cecil and BIFF–BANG–WALLOP went Cecil, swinging his fists at the bees. But the bees were too s–m–a–l–l to be walloped.

That *was* Amanda's Plan.

The biff–bang–walloping was no good at all.

Off went Cecil with the bees after him, hopping over Drumaness and Castlewellan and breaking a bit off Slieve Bernagh as he leapt over the Mournes (that's how Bernagh got its broken top), heading somewhere in the direction of Dundalk.

'Oh well done, Amanda!' said Mrs Ogle, patting tiny Amanda on the head. 'Hold on!' said all the peasants, coming out of hiding. 'What about our honey? And our bees! They've *gone*!'

'You ungrateful lot!' said Mrs Ogle, and she climbed up on the cow-cart and told Amanda to drive off to somewhere where there would be no *bees*.

'*You* decide where to, Amanda,' said Mrs Ogle.

'Oh, Ma!' moaned Amanda.

And Omagh is where they went!

(There *are* no 'B's in O-M-A-G-H!)